CONDITIONS
& CULPRITS

SONNY MARCH

SONNY MARCH

Edited by Gillian Dowell

Cover design by Mitch Green
@radstudio.co

radpublishing.co

This book is a work of fiction. Names,
characters, places, and incidents either
are the products of the author's
imagination or are used fictitiously. Any
resemblance to actual persons, living or
dead, events or locales is entirely
coincidental.

ISBN: 979-8-7590-7113-6

TRIGGER WARNING

Violence, sexual assault, torture, abuse,
anxiety, death.

FOR ALL THOSE WHO'VE
SUFFERED BUT CONTINUE TO
PRESS FORWARD

Can you really know a person with only one
slice?
No.
That first layer is nothing but hidden
emotions, a barrier holding back what's truly
inside.
That second layer, that shows a little bit more
of what lies beneath the first.
But that third layer shows true colors.
The blood red colors. That's when they're
really opened up and you can see everything
clearly.

DOWN A RUSTY ROAD

Lilly used to be the popular one. A cute, attractive blonde, captain of the cheer squad, senior prom queen. She was the type of person that people were envious of.

Everyone wanted to be like Lilly.

She had parents who spoiled her with extravagant things. The nice car, top-of-the-line clothing, and all the things that the lower class wished they could afford. She had plans

.

to go to college, build a bright future, and her parents were going to pay for it all.

But everything took a turn three weeks after graduation, when she realized she was pregnant.

Lilly had gotten knocked-up graduation night when she fucked one of her classmates in the backseat of her car during the after-party. Her life felt shattered when that double-line displayed itself, telling her she was going to be a mother. After relaying the news to the father of her child, he immediately took off, disappearing without a trace. He wanted nothing to do with Lilly, or the child he'd planted inside her.

As the weeks went by, she grew tired and anxious, worried about what her parents would think of the situation she'd put herself in. She dreaded telling them something that she knew they wouldn't approve of. Her mother and father were the type of people with no care for anyone but themselves, who thought they were better than everyone else. They would belittle someone right to their face, and their entitled opinions were now what she feared.

Lilly was an only child and was always handed everything she asked for, as well as the things that she didn't ask for. They never taught her how to be an adult. Lilly never had a job, never had responsibilities, and she solely relied on the backs of her parents—parents that she didn't want to disappoint for fear of losing everything.

The days were growing shorter and her belly began to protrude. Hiding it was no longer an option. Three months into her pregnancy, she finally told them, and just as she expected, they disowned her and treated her as if she were worthless. They took her car, her cellphone, everything they had given her except the clothes on her back, and kicked her out the door to fend for herself.

The absence of care and comfort were replaced by the first crutch offered to her, by the first generous man with selfish intentions. One hit, no second thoughts, and she found security in the loss of a sober mind.

Thirteen months after that positive test and numerous drug addictions later, Lilly wound up living in a small camper trailer off a dirt road, fourteen miles from the nearest city. It was July 11th, the peak of summer, when she locked herself in the tiny bathroom and away from her crying child, ignoring the fact that her son was sitting in his filthy diaper and desperate to be fed.

Meth sores covered nearly every part of her face and most of her teeth were decayed and broken. She stared into the mirror of the medicine cabinet, eyeing her naked self. What was once model material, was now sickly and pale.

Lifting her hand, she dug her thumbnail underneath the scab that was below her bottom lip, and peeled away the skin. Bloody puss oozed from the open pore, and began seeping down her chin and flowing down her neck. After wiping away the traces with a piece of toilet paper, she tossed the dirty tissue on the floor and opened the medicine cabinet. Grabbing a plastic tube of hemorrhoid cream off the shelf, she squeezed a quarter-sized amount onto her finger tips, then smeared it between her boney asscheeks in hopes of relieving the discomfort of her prolapsed anus. Having multiple dicks shoved daily into her rear by toothless drug dealers was the only way she could pay for her nasty addiction. As uncomfortable as it was, she sat down on the toilet seat and grabbed her crack pipe from the sink, grateful for the small bit of crystals inside that still remained from her stash.

She held her knees together and leaned her head slightly forward, pressing the glass to her lips, eager to fill her lungs with that precious smoke. Only being able to get one hit, it wasn't nearly enough to keep her sustained for very long. She needed more and she had no care in the world except making sure her high didn't wear off before she got her next fix.

Lilly left her trailer at 3:15 that afternoon, naked and intoxicated beneath the sun that was sweltering and in the temperature that was continuing to rise. The nearest drug den was three miles away, and after her beat-up Pinto wouldn't start, she took off walking down the long, dirt road. Behind her she pulled along a filthy old wagon that held her four-month-old child. Every rock, bump, and dip in the road caused the corroded carriage to jolt and metal shards to scrape her son's supple skin. Blisters were quickly beginning to form on his belly from being scorched by the heat of the sun. His poor, innocent soul was lying in a rusted frying pan, being ignored by his own selfish mother. She was deaf to the screaming of her child, consumed by the methamphetamine that she'd smoked less than two hours before. Sweat was dripping from her face and the soles of her bare feet were being lacerated by the rocks on the road. She was numb to the pain of it all, the voices in her mind telling her that she could be rewarded with consumable escapes if only she pressed on.

Lilly's head began to spin, dizziness adding to the spastic beating of her abused and exhausted heart. Halfway to her destination she went into cardiac arrest, falling face first into the ground. She died alongside her child, who passed away shortly after from choking on his own vomit.

Their bloated bodies sat out in the sun for days. Flies had laid eggs into their open mouths and maggots crawled in and out of their leathered nostrils. The distinctive smell of their rotting flesh attracted the carnivorous beasts that dragged away their carcasses into an open hayfield. Vultures picked apart their mutilated bodies, their bones were scattered by the animals that feasted on them, and no traces were left of Lilly and her child's tragic end except for that old, rusted wagon.

Two weeks went by before anyone traveled down that country road. The rainy days before had washed away any remaining blood that surrounded the horrific scene. A local farmer stopped when he noticed the abandoned wagon. He hopped out of his pickup and loaded it into his truck bed, excited about the treasure he'd just found. He planned to refurbish the wagon for his grandchildren that he loved and cared for; children that weren't suffering from the neglect of their parents.

They would ride in that dolled-up wagon that was being driven away down that dusty path out in the middle of nowhere. They would find joy and make childhood memories in what Lilly had carried behind her, pulling her and her legacy down the road she should have avoided.

A future could have been chosen that was brighter than the summer day that put an end to misery. Other decisions could have been made that could have proved worth in the woman that was cast away as worthless.

Lilly used to be somebody, but now she was a body that no one bothered to search for.

UNDER THE SKIN

You know the irritation that a single word can cause? A single sentence, single look, single comment on something entirely unnecessary?

Something singular and specific that drives right through the surface and penetrates the nerves.

That's all it took.

It was three o'clock in the afternoon and I stood there looking out the sliding glass doors from behind the counter, watching a drug addict rummaging through the ash tray out in front of the hotel. I found it pleasing to the eyes to see him smile after finding a half-smoked cigarette that he scored while digging through it like a fucking trash rat. It was amusing to me, but I also found it very interesting. Twenty-eight years old, and never once had I tried smoking. I never could understand what was so appealing about it, why someone would purposely want to char their own lungs. But what I do understand is that we all have our addictions, our wants, our desires. Things that we can't get enough of. Things that we can't stop even if we wanted to. And it doesn't always make sense to others why we do the things we do, but there's almost always a story, a reason, a purpose behind our actions.

I worked as a custodian the majority of the time, but often times they had me do a variety of different tasks if we were short-handed.

Sometimes they'd put me at the front desk—
that was my least favorite. Sitting up there and
having to welcome every asshole that came
into that place was not what I preferred,
because I wasn't a very social person. Roaming
around those dimly lit halls, cleaning dirty bed
sheets, taking out the trashes, and basically
handling all the general maintenance of things
around the hotel was far more entertaining
than standing in one place for hours. I didn't
mind getting my hands filthy, I actually really
enjoyed it. I enjoyed a lot of things about this
job, but what I didn't like, though, was some of
the small-minded, entitled pricks that came in
there on a weekly basis; burrowing mites that
liked to get underneath the skin of others. And
working at the front desk, I was forced to have
to put up with them. But I came up with the
perfect remedy, my own way of handling those
types of people, while at the same time

satisfying my own addiction, my own wants, and my own inner desires.

"Hi. How can I help you?"

"My wife and I have a reservation for the deluxe suite," he said as he stood there like a moron with his arm around his wife, acting as if they owned the fucking place.

The deluxe suite, the most expensive suite in the hotel. It wasn't as luxurious as it sounded, not in a small-town hotel like this one. It was more just an excessive way for assholes to throw out their money for show, to sleep in a bed with an insignificant amount of extra space when they're just going to be on top of and inside of whoever they're sleeping with, anyway. No one ever needs the extra space, the small details that only that suite possesses; like curtains that differ in color from the other hundred rooms, or a nicer view from their window that overlooks the grimy pool instead of the parking lot. It's just one more annoying way for someone—like him—to toss around their status.

"Okay, what's the name?" I asked.

"Are you fucking kidding me? I've been coming in here on the first of every month for the last eight months. You guys should know this by now."

Of course I knew who they were. They thought they were special, they thought they were a couple of small-town celebrities, but I wasn't going to entertain them by letting him know that I knew that. I wasn't going to feed their egos.

"No, not kidding you. So, can I get a name?"

"This is fucking ridiculous!" he shouted.

I stood there with a blank stare as I listened to the coward go on and on for several minutes. If only he knew how stupid he looked when he tried to look intimidating. His eyes were too wide to look threatening, and the fist he banged upon the counter to punctuate his words as he spoke was far too animated. But it didn't keep him from getting the attention he wanted, I noticed, as my manager turned the corner.

"Excuse me, what's the problem?" my manager asked.

"Your employee, that's the problem," he retorted. "I'm trying to get the keys to my room, but your employee here thinks it's funny to pretend like he doesn't know who the fuck I am."

"I apologize, Mr. and Mrs. Harris. Right this way," my manager gestured.

And just before they grabbed their bags and walked off, that's when it happened. That one thing that really got to me, the thing that I wasn't going to let go of—the thing that wasn't forgettable.

"Let's hope that your little brain can remember who I am the next time I come in here, if they haven't fired your incompetent ass by then."

No, it wasn't just that comment that came out of Mr. Harris's mouth, it was also the dirty, evil smirk on his wife's face that she gave me after causing a scene to get their way.

That's what got under my skin.

But what they didn't know was that I was a much bigger deal around that town than they were, and they weren't the only ones that knew how to play that game. I knew how to play it, too, but I was actually good at it. I may have started that game with only a quick moment's feigned ignorance, but the exchange wasn't over yet.

From one job to another. Making preparations was something that I was used to. It was no different than my work at the hotel. Cleaning my shop rags was no different than cleaning the pillow cases that were stained with drool and semen, swapping out my hacksaw blades after every use was no different than replacing the mop heads, unclogging my shop drain of clumps was no different than digging wads of hair out of the tub drains. It was a dirty job, but one that I was happily willing to do. The only difference from this job and my job at the hotel was that it didn't pay cash, but it did pay substantially in other ways.

Gratification.

But not all preparations were the same. Cleaning was just the first step, the most tedious of duties. Then came the easy part: following her. Well, all of them were easy parts, following her was just a simple part, just dull. Monday: yoga, where I watched her slowly and pointlessly move around and never even break a sweat. Tuesday: brunch with friends, where they all sat around over half-eaten meals and watered-down drinks while they gossiped about the most pathetic shit I'd ever eavesdropped on. Wednesday: nail appointment, when she spent an outrageous amount of money to change paint colors from teal to red. All the typical things you'd expect from a prissy little bitch. Thursday nights, those were her late-night jogging sessions, which worked out well for me because it just so happened to be my night off. That's the day I struck, struck that smirk right off her face with a ball-peen hammer. The only one smiling then, was me.

I had let that stupid remark that Mr. Harris made churn in my mind for two whole weeks before I did anything about it. I always found it best to let those things simmer for a while, because once that final moment finally came around and I did make my move, it was that much more fulfilling after the constant anticipation.

I sat in my fold-out chair above her sticky corpse, holding the ideal tool in the palm of my hands, the maple handles fit perfectly in my grip. I found it at the antique mall downtown and I couldn't pass it up. It was buried beneath a pile of blacksmithing tools just waiting for its rightful owner, someone like me who would appreciate such a fine piece of steel. It was a rusted old thing, but it still had a very good edge on it. Most would say it was junk, but I took one look at it and just had to have it. With proper care I would make it last a lifetime.

With her leg propped up on the table in front of me, I mounted the blade of the drawknife just below her kneecap, and with one fluid stroke along the shin, I produced a perfect fillet. Her limbs were dainty, there wasn't much there, but I was still able to peel a little satisfaction. I sliced off the end of her flesh just at the ankle bone and tossed it into a metal bucket that sat on the floor beside me. I lifted my arm to wipe the sweat from my brow, smearing streaks of red across my forehead. It was hot and muggy in my garage. The box fan sitting in the corner was the only thing supplying me with a small bit of cool air while I continued my task.

What a waste of time; not what I was doing, but what she'd been doing. All that effort she spent pampering herself and catering to her looks when I personally thought she looked much better this way—mutilated and stuck to my concrete slab. I felt it especially accentuated her beautiful bone structure. If only her husband could see the way she looked then. I thought of snapping a few photos and sending them his way, but that seemed a little generous. What I'd already had in mind was more than enough.

I pushed her foot off the table and stood up from the chair with my bucket of goodies in hand. I walked over to my work bench, leaving bloody shoe prints behind with every step I took. Reaching into the bucket, I grabbed a slimy handful of pieces, then sprawled them out on a baking sheet before me: fingers and toes that I had snipped off with wire cutters, her eyes that I had dug out with a serrated knife, and those fillets that my precious drawknife shaved off her bones with very little effort. I left her gaudy fingernails attached; it was the least I could do, considering she had just had them done the day before, and I wasn't sure if Mr. Harris had had a chance to see them yet. I wanted to remind him of how his money that he cared so much for was being spent.

After coiling all of her severed parts tightly into a bundle of her own flesh and creating a human wrap, I packed it all into a plastic bubble mailer and left it on her husband's doorstep later that night, saving one, small, perfectly squared piece of her skin for myself before disposing of her mangled body.

To think that a man like Mr. Harris would call a man like me incompetent. Would an incompetent man have the skills and knowledge to craft a plan this devious? Would he be capable of being cunning enough to win a game like this? *Incompetent.* What an ironic word for a man like him to throw around.

The next day I received the local paper and on the front page was an article showcasing my accomplishment.

Husband receives anonymous package of his wife's severed body parts.

Serial killer strikes again.

The investigation continues.

This is a red-flag warning for all those living inside and outside of city limits. Be aware of your surroundings and please contact the authorities immediately if you have any suspicions, or any information regarding the missing persons reports. Please remain calm and don't panic, as we are working tirelessly to find the person responsible for these horrific acts.

I clipped out the article and hung it up on my wall just above her piece of skin that I had preserved alongside the seven other works of art that were displayed in my garage. My collection was quickly growing and I couldn't be more enthralled by it. Each one a story. A reason. A purpose.

I sat parked in the hotel's lot with the window down just waiting for my shift to start with the unfamiliar smoke spilling from the cancerous stick between my fingers. I'd grabbed a pack on my way to work, wanting to try out someone else's addiction for a change. It only took one taste to know it wasn't for me, to know it wouldn't quite be what quenched the kind of craving that I lived with and regularly satiated. If the appeal of these disgusting things was the slow and painful death they were notorious for, then it wasn't worth it. There were better ways, ones that brought more satisfaction and accomplishments, and I smiled as I thought of them while I walked to the front door, ready to clock into the work that I loved—but not more than my real job. Not more than the career that made me who I was, that made me bigger than most; bigger than that egotistical widower could ever be.

"Here." Only one cigarette was missing from the pack I offered to the guy once again rummaging through the ash tray, desperate for a fix of his addiction. So simple, so stupid.

"For real? Thanks, man! You're a lifesaver!"

I wouldn't go as far as considering myself a lifesaver. I was a life taker and I had only given him the proper tools to shorten his own life himself.

Once again we were under-staffed and they put me in charge of the front desk. Another day, another asshole. I stood there looking at the computer screen in front of me when he walked up to the counter. And as I pretended not to see him standing there, he repeatedly pressed on the service bell until I turned my head in his direction.

"Oh, hi, didn't see you there. How can I help you?"

"Do you have a hearing problem or something? I've been standing here for well over three minutes. I have a reservation."

"Okay, what's the name?" I asked—even though I knew who he was.

"Seriously?"

I was an expert at purposely trying to agitate people—although I wouldn't suggest that you do the same, because you may fall short and come across someone like me. A serial murderer. A skin collector. A man who has no problem kidnapping and butchering another man's wife. But if you do go around intentionally trying to irritate someone, at least do it the right way.

To get under someone's skin, my best advice is to send them a piece of their spouse's.

HOME REMEDIES

My mind was spinning in circles as I stared at the clock, waiting for the doctor to come into the examination room. I was preparing myself for the terrible news that I knew I was about to receive.

It was my third time visiting that week. I still felt that there was something seriously wrong with me. I had cancer, I just knew it. The worst kind, too, the untreatable kind. The fucking cancer that is slow and painful, the same type of cancer that my best friend had suffered through and died of less than two months back.

I weighed in at a scrawny one hundred and eleven pounds—seven pounds down from the week prior. I had every symptom, I read about them online. Weight loss. Loss of appetite. Aches and pains. Headaches. Difficulty breathing. Fatigue.

I was only twenty-two years old; I wasn't ready to die.

"Hey, Victor, how are we doing today?" the doctor asked as he walked into the room.

"Not good."

"Okay, well, let's take a look at ya."

He sat down on the rolling stool in front of me and I closely watched his facial expressions as he held the stethoscope up to my chest and told me to take a deep breath. His firm eyebrows had me questioning his thoughts as he was listening to my rapid heartbeat. The look on his face made me believe that there was definitely going to be some bad news fixing to spill out of his mouth, which would send me into an immediate panic attack.

"So, tell me, Victor. What is the reason for your visit today?"

"I keep having these pains in the left side of my stomach. I'm very concerned. They won't go away."

"Well, if you've been digging your fingers into your side the way you are right now, then I can see why the muscles might be a little sore. I've already told you several times, Victor, you're perfectly healthy. There is no reason for you to worry. We've given you every test. We've tested your blood, tested your urine, you had a CT scan, X-rays, a colonoscopy. They all came back clear. It's just your anxiety."

"That's what you keep telling me, but I feel that it's more than just that. And it's been very hard for me to get any sleep at night, because I'm so worried that there's something you guys are overlooking."

"Anxiety can cause you to believe that there is something wrong with you, Victor. But I assure you that there is nothing physically wrong."

Telling me that I have severe anxiety didn't help me at all. Trying to put me on medication to calm my nerves didn't help me, either. I refused to take them. I was too paranoid about the side-effects of those drugs. What if they were to fuck me up worse than I already was? Even though I felt a slight bit of relief once the doctor had told me that there was nothing wrong with me, it still didn't stop me from being worried that there actually was. It didn't stop me from immediately getting back on my phone and looking stuff up online. And I felt that so long as the doctors were getting paid, that they didn't give a shit about my well-being. It's like they never listened, and it was frustrating.

Why I even went to the hospital in the first place, I don't know. I guess it was fear that kept me going back. Fear that told me I would likely die if I didn't, fear that they fed on and profited from. And after that visit I swore to myself that I wouldn't go back and that from then on, I'd just self-diagnose. I knew my body better than they did.

To hell with their doctorate.

I prescribed myself a remedy: watching countless hours of porn. It was my meditation; a way to divert my mind into a different direction—to relieve my suffering. I would glue my eyes to the computer screen and scroll through porn sites, clicking on numerous videos until I found the right one.

Some days I would do it for hours. I would masturbate until it felt like my balls had been beaten with a hammer. But as soon as the pain would subside, I would go right back at it.

It quickly became an addiction.

For the hundredth time within weeks, I sat in my desk chair watching tits bounce and stroked myself for the seventh time that day. My glass of ice water sat next to me at arm's length and I took sips from it every few minutes to stay hydrated.

It fueled me to keep going.

One hand on my dick and the other on the touchpad. I clicked on the search column and browsed the content to find the video that I had in mind. It was one that I'd already seen many times before; one that I knew didn't take much to turn me on and get me off.

There it was.

I lined up the cursor and clicked the play button. I turned the volume up as the erotic show began rolling and leaned back in my chair as my mind soaked up everything my eyes were seeing.

As I picked up the pace, stroking my chafed shaft despite the excruciating pain, a breathless yell escaped my lungs as my body spit out fluids into the sock that had been resting on my thigh, waiting for its fill.

Curling forward with my eyes tightly shut, I put my forehead to the edge of the wooden desk. I sat there motionless, listening to the moaning sounds of the video coming through the laptop speakers, then opened my eyes to the sight of bloodied semen staining through the white cotton.

Panic immediately set in.

It was embarrassing to have to tell the nurse what had happened and why I was back, not even three weeks having passed since my last visit. She sat there logging all the information of my anxiety-induced incident onto her clipboard before leaving the examination room.

I could hear snickering in the hallway, knowing that her and all her colleagues were getting a good laugh out of my unfortunate situation. I sat on the end of the table, caught up in my silent thoughts and feeling even more depressed than the last time I was here.

After fifteen minutes had gone by, the doctor finally walked into the room with an idiotic smirk on his face.

"Sounds like you had an overdose," he said.

I sat there with a blank stare, showing no reaction to what he apparently thought was a humorous joke.

He reached out and handed me the orange plastic pill bottle. "You're going to be all right, Victor. Just take two of these a day, keep your hands off yourself, and you'll be good to go."

But I looked down at the label, and I could read the small print and see exactly what side-effects those small circles of chemicals could cause. Yet again, no help at all. Another wasted trip, another thirty-five-dollar copay, just to toss the bottle in the trash outside the hospital as I left.

There was no way I was going to expose my body to harmful synthetics.

His prescription was a risk that I wasn't willing to take.

I was just going to have to find my own remedy.

INHUMANE

"Put that shit away. You can finish your schoolwork another time. It's almost time to go," he said.

It was mid-October, hunting season, my father's favorite time of year. I was nervous, considering it was my first time. I didn't want to go, but he made me, he said that this was something I needed to learn, that this was what it took to keep food on the table and that it was more important than anything I could learn from a stupid textbook. I was home-schooled; he didn't trust the school system. He didn't like the fact that they taught their students the same unnecessary things back-to-back every single year. That wasn't the type of education he wanted for me. He'd always tell me that all it took to make it in the real world was hard work and common sense, which was something I couldn't disagree with. Often times I questioned some of the lessons he taught, though, because not all of them made sense to me. But I was only nine years old and he was the only person I had around to rely on, look up to, and go to if I needed answers for things that I didn't understand.

We lived in the country. I didn't have friends. I didn't have any other family. And I had only learned what he taught me, the things that he thought were important.

"You 'bout ready?"

"Almost. Just have to get my boots on," I said.

"Hurry up. I want to be out there four hours before sun down. You have five minutes. I'll be out in the truck waiting. Don't make me come back into this house. Understood?"

"Yeah."

"It's 'yes, sir' when you're talking to me." He stared down at me with his hateful demeanor as I sat on the floor, slipping on my boots as he waited for a response.

"Yes, sir," I said. And I cowered down to his words.

My nerves grew even more uncontrollable after seeing that rifle slung over his shoulder as he walked out the door. We spent the last two weeks target practicing in the backyard. Three boxes of ammunition after being cursed at, smacked around, and being called a moron twenty times before I was able to get it right. He said we couldn't afford to miss a shot.

"God dammit, Clay! Are you that fucking stupid? It's not that hard, dumbass. If you'd stop shaking maybe you could hit the target," he'd said.

But it was difficult to stop myself from shaking when I was terrified of being abused, terrified of his outbursts, terrified of the hunting trip all together. Shooting a target was much different than shooting something living and real. I didn't know if I had the heart to kill innocent creatures.

The wilderness was a peaceful place. It was calm. The air was crisp. The colors of the leaves that covered the ground were nothing short of spectacular. I watched as squirrels gathered acorns that had fallen from the surrounding oak trees. I spent time in my thoughts while listening to the soothing sounds of nature. I soaked up all there was to see and hear, hoping that nothing would come across our paths that day that would force me to pull that trigger, but just as the sun began to set, that's when an opportunity presented itself, an opportunity that I didn't want to take.

"Dad, I have to pee."

"Shhh. Hold it, Clay!" he whispered harshly. "Look," he pointed.

I wish I hadn't seen it. I wasn't the same person that my father was. Killing came easily to him, maybe it was because it wasn't his first time and that he'd grown numb to it. My father thought he was right about everything, and even though I thought this was terrible, that this was inhumane, I wouldn't dare tell him that he was wrong. He was a very hateful and abusive man, and telling him that he was wrong would only lead to me getting beaten, lashed with a belt—or worse, he'd lock me in the cellar again; that place where I starved for almost two days before he'd come back and let me out. And for what? For trying to fight back after he'd held me down and banged my head against the floor for back-talking? Torture was inevitable, but this time I got to decide where it was directed. It didn't have to be me.

"Calm down, Clay. Stop shaking and keep it steady. Take a deep breath and take your time. Line up the crosshairs just like we've practiced, and when you're ready, pull the trigger," he whispered.

And just like that, I became a killer.

The gunshot echoed through the forest, squirrels quickly scurried to their nests, and what was once a peaceful place had turned into a dark memory that was going to live in my mind for the rest of my life.

Those beautiful autumn leaves were now covered in blood. My heart was pounding in my chest and I was overwhelmed with a rush of emotions. My eyes began to water as I felt sadness for the soul dying at my feet, watching it as it struggled to breathe. Its glossy eyes were open wide and looking directly at me. I couldn't help to wonder what it was thinking. *Why did you shoot me? Why are you doing this? Please help me.*

"Good job, son. I'm proud of you," my father said as he reached down and put his hand on my shoulder.

Those words that he spoke to me in that moment were words that I'd never heard him say before. That was the very first time he'd told me he was proud of me, and it wasn't very often that he even referred to me as his son. He'd always called me by my name; a name that was picked out by my mother, long before I was born.

Working with ceramics was her passion, and I guess that's where the name Clay came from. I know my mother had her own room in the house that held all of her greatest pieces; it was her sanctuary, where her mind wandered and her creativity soared. The shelves had been filled with a lifetime's worth of her crafted art.

The peace of that room died with her.

It was a sanctuary for no one any longer, and all those shelves now stood empty after my father shattered every single thing she'd ever made. I was always instructed not to enter that room, not to ruin the only thing he had left of her. One by one, each bout of anger resulted in the destruction of her memory. When there were no more things to break, nothing breakable in that room left to turn to, he started on her last and only remaining creation.

Me.

In my father's eyes, I was the one to blame. After she died giving birth to me, I was nothing to him but a worthless disappointment.

"It's getting dark, Clay. Don't just stand there, grab the knife that I bought you. It's time you put it to use."

I got down on my knees with the blade in my hand, and held back my tears as my father watched me intently. As hard as it was to stomach after what I'd already done, I made a small incision in the lower part of its belly, then stuck two fingers into the cut, just as he'd instructed, proceeding to tug up on the skin and slice all the way up the midline to the breastbone, making sure I wasn't puncturing any of the internal organs.

"Now you're going to have to stick your hands in and pull everything out."

"I don't want to. I can't." My voice shook, just like the rest of me.

He reached down and wrapped his hand around the back of my neck, and looked me directly in the face with his menacing eyes. "You can, and you will. I don't care about what you want. You're gonna do what I fucking tell you to."

He pushed me forward, placing me a breath away from the carcass in front of me. Looking away again wasn't an option. Pulling back wasn't, either.

The stern look on his face was enough to frighten every bone in my body, and I knew there was no way out of this, so I rolled up the sleeves of my camouflage shirt and stuck my small hands into the open cavity. Warm blood covered my arms all the way up to my elbows as I gripped my fingers around all the entrails and yanked everything out onto the ground in front of me, then I used my knife to cut away all that was attached until the cavity was completely hollow.

"That's enough," my father said as he grabbed hold of the ankles and stood. "Let's go."

As he walked away, dragging the gutted, lifeless thing behind him, I took the chance to quickly wipe my bloodied hands on the ground while he wasn't looking.

I stood to my own feet, despite the shakiness, and reached down to grab my knife.

For a second, I debated on leaving it there, on never touching it again and forgetting what I'd done with it. But then I thought of the consequences that would come of it. What would happen if he knew that I'd left something so important just lying in the woods. If he thought I'd done so carelessly.

I picked it up, and turned to see my father look over his shoulder at me. One stern tip of his head—an unspoken order—and I rushed to catch up.

The night-drive home was silent, not a word was spoken. But silence was better than the lecture that I'd expected from him. And a lecture was the least of my worries.

Once we'd gotten back to the house, my father backed the truck up to the pole barn just in front of the gambrel where we hung the carcass upside down by its ankles.

It was time for the skinning process, the one thing I was dreading most. I'd watched my father do it several times in the past. He'd strip away the skin until all the muscle tissue was exposed, then he'd quarter up the body using a hacksaw and continue butchering, cutting meat from the bones and grinding it all up.

I had always watched from a distance. It was a disturbing and unsettling thing to witness, but even more terrible now that I was forced to take part in it and see everything up close. I didn't know how much more of it I was going to be able to handle before I completely lost myself and broke down.

"Get your ass inside and get cleaned up. I've had enough out of you." His hateful tone penetrated my ears, but I couldn't be more relieved by the fact that he didn't make me stand there and help him finish.

I quickly ran inside, stripped off my clothes, and hopped in the shower—my first moment of freedom since we'd left the house, the first moment that I was able to express the way I felt. Tears fell from my eyes as I thought back to everything I'd done that night, and what my father was outside continuing to do as I was scrubbing away the blood off my arms and watching it fall to the bottom of the tub. Even though the soap and water physically washed everything away, I still had blood on my hands. I still had to live with the guilt. I still felt that this was wrong. And nothing about it made sense to me.

After stepping out of the shower and drying myself off, I looked into the mirror and was mortified, disappointed in myself. I couldn't get over it and tears began to fill my eyes once again. But I was fixing to walk out of the bathroom and couldn't allow my father to see me this way, so I grabbed the towel from the rack and wiped away the sadness. As I opened the door to head to my bedroom, I heard that punishing voice holler my name from the backyard.

"Clay!"

I looked out the screen door on the back of the house. He was sitting under the stars in his old, beat-up lawn chair. His silver-white hair peeked out beneath his camouflage cap, he had a beer in his bloody hand, and he was listening to classic rock music blaring through the radio speakers that were mounted in the shed. He was calm, too calm, as if nothing about what had happened that night had fazed him in the slightest.

"Come here," he demanded.

I stepped out the back door, walked over to where he sat, and he looked up at me when he noticed the redness in my eyes.

"What's wrong with you, boy?" I might have thought in that moment that he actually cared if it weren't for the scowl he had on his face.

"What we did wasn't right." I took a leap of courage and spoke exactly what was on my mind only to be shut down.

"I don't care about what you think is right, Clay. You need to learn and understand."

"Yeah, but—"

"But nothing!" He shook his head in disappointment. "God dammit, Clay! He was not innocent! That man you shot tonight was an animal, and he got what he fucking deserved." He turned in his seat, unable to look at me any longer. His stare was distant, directed toward the trees. "He trespassed on our land, Clay!" He tossed his beer can to the ground, and in the same moment I sucked in my breath I felt some relief that it wasn't me he took out his aggression on.

"If they go around killing our wildlife, then we won't have food on the table. I'm going to tell you one more time, Clay: they're all animals.

And if you ever tell anyone about this, I'll hang you up by your fucking baby toes and I'll do to you what I did to him. Understood?"

"Yes, sir."

"Good. Now run along to bed, because tomorrow we have more work to do."

I stayed awake, looking up at the ceiling, crying, wishing that all of it was just a dream, but it wasn't. I had to live with what I'd done. I tried to talk myself down from the guilt by telling myself that things could be worse, that my father could make me eat the man that I killed. The thought of devouring human meat made me want to vomit. Sometimes I'd wonder if I hadn't already had a taste of human flesh and my father just didn't tell me about it. It wasn't something that I'd put past him.

I pulled the covers over my head, and gripped my pillow as tight as I could to comfort myself from the pain and heartache that I felt, and that's when the suicidal thoughts began to kick in. I was so anxious about the next day, but I thought that if I just killed myself then I wouldn't have to worry about what was yet to come, I wouldn't have to live a life of guilt— and I wouldn't have to put up with any more abuse. As the overwhelming thoughts took over my mind, my eyes began to close, but the images in my head didn't cease until I finally dozed off.

The next morning, I woke up to the bright sunlight shining through my bedroom windows. I lay there in bed not wanting to get up from it to face my father, but if I had stayed there for too long, then it would've only been a matter of time before he'd barge into my room to wake me up anyway.

After building up the courage to finally get up, I walked out from my bedroom and into the living room where my father was always sitting, every morning, watching television. He sat too still. He was silent when normally he would have already had a harsh command for me, some chore to do or expectation to meet laced with as many insults or curses as he could manage. But he said nothing, his eyes closed when they should have already been open and looking forward to the day's work.

I walked timidly to the chair, ready for him to jump angrily awake at any second. By the time I set my palm to his wrist, ready to shake him awake, I knew there was more wrong with his silence.

Nothing thumped beneath my hand, nothing pulsed beneath his skin. No heartbeat, no pulse like he'd taught me how to wait out in a dying *animal*. I would learn that it was a heart attack, a swift but painful way out for him, but in that moment, I wasn't concerned with 'how'.

For the first time I was alone, and I had to think for myself.

There was no command for me to follow, nobody to teach me or answer my questions.

What was I supposed to do now?

What would happen to me, a child now alone?

And why was I sad? After all the abuse, after the very day before where my hand was forced and guilt still consumed me, why would his death matter?

He was my father. Despite it all, despite his lack of nurturing and capability to be good, it mattered because he mattered.

He was all I'd had.

Twenty years later, I sat in that very same spot, on that very same day in October, on the land that I inherited—a place that I never thought

I'd again step foot on—and I thought back to the horrible things that my father made me do. All those years had passed and I thought about how no one had ever found the remains of the men that he murdered or the man that I was forced to kill that night. He must have done a good job of covering things up, because nothing ever came of it. But I never once told a soul about what had happened; my last and only gift to my father, which I would take to my grave.

"Dad, look," he whispered. "Do you see it?"

The excitement on his face was much different than the terrifying look that I'd had on my face the last time I was out here.

"I do." I smiled. "You got this. Take a deep breath and take your time. And when you're ready, take the shot," I whispered.

Click

My heart started pounding when I heard it, and then I realized I had said something so close to the same thing that my father had said to me all those years ago.

But this time it was different.

"What do you think, dad?" He lifted his hand, handing me the camera that displayed a beautiful white-tail deer on the LCD screen.

"That's a great photo, son. Your mother is going to love that one." I smiled.

"Are you okay, dad?" He looked up at me with concern as he saw the tears beginning to fall from my eyes.

"Yes, son." I was. Everything was finally okay. I could give to my son the care of a father that I was never given by my own. "I just love you, and I'm just so proud of you."

FUNNEL CAKE

It was exceptionally slow that night, more so than it was most nights. The place sat on the top of a hill and looked like a rundown farmhouse. I ordered my drink and sat in the same booth as I did every Thursday for the last month. Every so often I made a change in scenery to keep things interesting, and to remain unnoticed for the sake of the nights meant for more than just observing.

The lights were always dim. The women in the strip club were typically grotesque. They walked about, fully nude, and offered lap dances for as little as a buck. Funnel cakes, that's what I call them. They're greasy and sometimes unappealing, but they are oh so sweet and addictive once you get a taste. Every week I saw new faces, new employees, different titties, and different asses. I preferred the thicker ones, myself, but that night I had my eyes on a cute, skeletal brunette. Aside from her being bone skinny, she had a lot of other great physical features. She had long, curly hair, gorgeous brown eyes, a pretty smile and clear skin—not to mention her beautiful collar bones. She was unlike the rest, who were mostly covered in track marks. I wondered why a girl like her was working in a place like this. She was a girl that I wouldn't mind getting my dick sucked by, but that's not why I was there.

Having my dick sucked wasn't a high priority, it wasn't the only thing that I enjoyed that got me off.

"Hey, sweetie. What's your name?" she asked.

She sat down on the edge of the table and I took a sip of my beverage. I looked up at her big bright eyes and she smiled down at me as she waited for me to respond. I never gave out my real name. I had a list of names to choose from that I would often use anytime someone would ask me that question.

"Oliver."

"Nice to meet you, Oliver. I'm Cassandra. People around here call me Cassy, but you can call me whatever you'd like." She smiled. "Would you like a lap dance?"

"I'm all right, thanks." I forced an uninterested look on my face, but internally, I was lit up with anticipation.

"Oh, come on, are you sure? You're pretty handsome. I won't even make you pay for it."

"I'm sure."

"Okay, hun, well if you change your mind, you know where to find me. I'll be here until eleven o'clock." She winked, hopped down off the table, and walked away.

I looked down when I noticed that her sweaty asscheeks left an imprint on the table where she had sat down. I ran my fingertips across the smooth surface, across that little grease mark, and secretly lifted them to my mouth and grazed them across my tongue. She tasted heavenly. She was a sweet little funnel cake, but that tiny sample wasn't enough to satisfy my appetite. I wanted more. I needed more. She was going home with me that evening—whether she was willing or not.

I sat waiting in my vehicle in the unlit parking lot just outside the strip club, and I watched the front doors until I saw my little beauty walk out of the building, glowing beneath the small, colorful neon sign that hung above the front entrance. She was fully dressed this time, unlike before. She had on a tight, black mini-skirt and a white tank-top, but it didn't matter what she had on, I planned on removing all of her clothing before the night was over with.

She reached into her purse and grabbed her keys, then began walking across the gravel lot. As she moved closer to passing by my vehicle, I rolled down my window.

"Hey, miss."

She stopped and looked towards me.

"Oh, hey! Oliver, right?"

"Yes, that's right."

"Were you waiting on me out here?" The playful grin on her face told me she was just as delighted to see me as I was to see her.

"Actually, I was." I laughed. "I didn't want to go back inside, and you had told me you were getting off work soon. I was waiting because I just wanted to apologize for earlier. I know I came off as a little rude. It's been a frustrating day, but I didn't mean to take it out on you. So, I'm sorry for that."

"Oh, it's fine, hun, I didn't think anything of it." She smiled.

"Hey, tell you what, if you're not doing anything right now, how about I make it up to you? Would you like to go for a late dinner?" I asked.

"Oh my god, yes! Please! I'm famished!" she said with enthusiasm.

It was much easier than I had anticipated. She willingly walked around to the passenger-side door and climbed into the vehicle, then we pulled away from the strip club and headed to the nearby diner.

"So tell me, Cassandra, why is a beautiful young woman like yourself working at a place like that?"

"You think I'm beautiful? Wow, with compliments like that I may just develop a real crush on you." She smiled. "I'm just working there to pay my way through college."

"Well, isn't there other job choices that are a lot less demeaning?" I asked.

"Are you judging me?"

"Oh, no. I meant no offense. I was just curious."

"I looked around for other jobs, but none of them paid well. Also, I'm very comfortable in my own skin and if some guy or girl wants to ogle my goodies for money, well, then I don't mind. It pays off."

"I will say, Cassandra, you do have some pretty nice goodies." I turned my head and gave her a sly grin.

"You're scoring all kinds of brownie points and I barely even know you." She smiled. "Do you charm all the ladies this way?"

"Only the cute ones."

It didn't take long before we arrived at the diner and we sat down at one of the high-top tables. The place was pretty empty considering how late it was, and there was only one old man, sitting in a booth alone, looking down at the newspaper he held in his wrinkly hands. The waitress gave us our menus and we gazed over them as she stood nearby, waiting for us to order.

"Hey, I know it's not on the menu, but you guys wouldn't happen to have funnel cakes, would you?" Cassandra asked.

My eyes lit up with excitement and my heart began thumping rapidly when I heard those words spill from her lips. I knew from that moment that I had made an excellent choice.

She may actually be the one, the one I have been waiting for—but only time would tell.

"I think we can fix that up for ya," the waitress replied.

"Great! Thanks, that's what I want."

"Sir, what about you? Are you ready to order?"

"Yeah, I'll just take a coffee," I said.

As we waited for the waitress to come back with our orders, we sat and I listened to her ramble on about her life. She told me how she came to be where she was now and where she grew up. Basically, she told me the short version of her whole life story. I paid no attention to half the things she said. I only had my mind on one thing and one thing only: getting her back to my house. And with the way things were looking, it didn't seem like it was going to be a very difficult thing to manage.

"One funnel cake, and one coffee. Can I get you guys anything else?"

"Nope, I think we're good," I answered.

I sat in silence and I watched closely as Cassandra devoured that plate of sweet, oily swirls and sucked the powdered sugar from her fingers after every bite. She seemed very pleased and I was also very pleased just watching her enjoy it as I sat there drinking my coffee.

"Do you want some, Oliver? It's *so* good."

"No, thanks."

"Okay, suit yourself."

After paying the check we walked out of the diner. I wasn't sure what my next move was going to be. I was never one to easily give up, though, so if I couldn't talk her into coming back to my house, then I would just have to force it upon her. But before we even made it to my vehicle, she said those perfect words, those words that presented the exact opportunity that I was looking for.

"So, are we going to your place or what?" she asked with a mischievous grin.

This had all been made very easy for me, the easiest time I'd had luring a woman back to my place. On the way there I thought about the filthy things I was going to do to Cassandra. I was already getting turned on by the thought of it, but I gave away no indication of my excitement.

"Wow. I love your house," she said.

"Thank you. Would you like a drink?"

"Sure, hook me up with something good. Surprise me."

She sat down on the sofa. I came back from the kitchen with two glasses of whiskey, sat hers down on the coffee table, and she picked up the glass before looking me in the eyes.

"You know, Oliver, you don't have to get me tipsy to fuck me."

I smiled and took a sip of my drink.

"Show me your bedroom, show me where the action happens," she said.

She didn't want to waste any time at all, and quite frankly, I didn't either. I was more than ready to have my way with her. It had been several hours of this piddling around nonsense.

"Right this way." I gestured.

We made our way down the hall to the farthest section of the house towards the back. I pushed open the door, turned on the light, and there displayed the room—the room with my table where I chain down my women and have my fun. I wasn't sure how she'd react once she'd seen that the only thing in that room was a video camera mounted on a tripod, one solid maple dresser, and my sex table, but the fact that she worked in a strip club made me think that she wouldn't be entirely opposed to it, either. So, I just took my chances and it worked out the way I'd wanted it to.

"Oh, so you like it kinky do ya?"

I stood in the doorway, shrugged my shoulders, and smiled.

"Well, you're in luck, Oliver, because I do too." She pulled her top off and my eyes naturally glanced down at her pointed nipples, then she turned around and bent herself over the table, lifting her mini-skirt to reveal the white silky panties hiding beneath it. She looked back at me and bit her bottom lip that still held small traces of powdered sugar from earlier. "So, do you want to strap me down and fuck me, Oliver? You can choose whatever hole you'd like."

She was in for a real surprise, because I had already made up my mind on which hole I was going to tear apart long before we even stepped foot into my house. I closed the door behind me and walked up behind her. Grabbing her small hips, I thrust myself against her as she let out a slight moan. She put her face down on the table and I reached over her, grabbed her wrists, then placed them in the cuffs that were fastened to the corners. I slowly ran my middle finger down her spine all the way to her tailbone, then slid aside her panties and pressed my dry finger into her ass.

"Oh my god, Oliver. Yes. Fuck me," she moaned.

I finger fucked her only for a few seconds while I watched her tight asshole grip the skin around my knuckle, then I moved my way down to her ankles and strapped them into the cuffs that were attached to the table legs, her feet still firmly planted on the floor. I pulled from my pocket a blindfold and tightened it around Cassandra's eyes. I walked over to the dresser and pulled out a pair of stainless-steel scissors, to snip away her underwear and toss them aside. I got down on my knees behind her and with both hands I grabbed hold of her small hips, shoved my face into the crack of her ass, and took one solid lick.

Finally, a second taste. Delectable. I savored it. I bathed in the flavor. I loved it.

"I'll be right back. Are you good?" I asked. I didn't actually care about how comfortable she was feeling, I was only giving her a false sense of security and letting her think that I was a kind person by asking her that simple question.

"God damn, Oliver. You're such a tease. Hurry up. I don't think I can wait another minute."

I was gone only long enough to grab my cardboard box of supplies. I came back into the room, locked the door behind me, and sat everything down on the floor.

"You're back," she said. "I'm so wet, Oliver, just fuck me already."

"Oh, it's coming, sweetheart, don't you worry. I'm going to give it to you real good, like you've never had it before."

"Please do," she said anxiously.

I slid onto my hands a pair of cowhide gloves, then reached into the box, pulling out a makeshift funnel I had fashioned out of an old, six-inch tin can. I had taken no care to smooth out its metal splinters, and it was already beginning to oxidize from its past uses. I stood behind her, watering my mouth before spitting a generous amount of my saliva between her boney crevice—not that it was going to do any good. Then I lined the tapered end of the jagged funnel right above her sphincter, and with no remorse, I shoved it into her ass. I pressed down on the top of it with my free hand to ensure that it was fully secure and not going to come loose once I'd let go. I twisted it in as far as I could and its sharp edges clung to the inside of her like a couple of miniature bait hooks. She let out a breathless cry, her knees buckled inward, and her body began shaking uncontrollably from the excruciating pain. Quickly reaching down, I pulled out a can of boiling vegetable oil from the box that had been heating on the burner in the kitchen ever since I'd made our drinks. I poured it into the funnel as urine and bloody grease flowed down her open thighs and dripped onto the floor beneath her feet. She lay there bent over, whimpering and twitching in agony, like a helpless squirrel that had just gotten hit by a vehicle on the road. And for the final touch, the icing on the cake, I dusted a handful of powdered sugar along the top edges of the metal rim. Slipping off my gloves, I unzipped my pants, and picked up her silky panties off the floor. I wrapped them around my hardened cock and started stroking myself off as blood bubbles began to form up through the funnel. As I watched the boiling liquid fry the inside of her rectum, I couldn't help but to let loose what I had been holding in this entire time. And just as I jacked off into the funnel and my fluids mixed with hers, her breathing stopped and her body went completely limp.

"Mmm. Fuck yeah," I groaned.

With her panties still wrapped around the base of my cock, I lay down on the floor and rested my head between her ankles. I closed my eyes as I let the greasy blood drip from her dirty cunt into my mouth, and I licked my lips and thought back to the very first taste of love.

Her name was Natalie. She was my one and only for several years. I still remembered the sweet taste of powdered sugar on her tongue from when I'd kiss her. I still remembered the smile on her face anytime I would whip up our favorite treat. I remembered all the long, tiring, late nights we spent together in the kitchen, frying batter to satisfy our addictive appetites. I'd thought she was my forever, but then she left me for another man, left me without a goodbye, without an explanation. It broke me. It murdered my sanity and killed my humanity. But I still loved her. And I missed her. Ever since then I'd had trouble finding one that tasted just as good as her love felt—nothing ever came close in comparison.

Cassandra was a delight, one of the best ones yet, but I still wasn't fully content. So I'd have to keep searching, searching for something sweeter, searching for the right one to satisfy my craving.

Searching for the perfect funnel cake.

SCREWED

John had only ever been under a house once before—his parents' house. He'd been helping his father install new water pipes and was in charge of holding the flashlight while he worked. He had also been in charge of making trips back and forth to the shed to grab supplies. His father was a heavy-set man and had trouble getting in and out of tight spaces, so it was easier for John to quickly squirm his way around, being the six-year-old little boy that he was.

He'd been having so much fun spending time with his father that day. He'd watched him closely while he worked, and thought about how he wanted to be just like him when he grew up. He wanted to learn everything he knew, know how to fix things, and be the capable handy-man that his father was. They'd spent hours underneath the house that day and John was enjoying every second of the adventure, but that adventure became a nightmare whenever he'd come back from making a trip to the shed and found his father face-down, lifeless on the ground. His father had tried to turn around to grab one of his tools from behind him, when a sharp piece of rebar sticking up from the soil stabbed into his leg and sliced open his femoral artery, and he'd quickly and fatally bled out.

It was one of the most traumatizing and unforgettable moments John had ever experienced.

The haunting memory of it all followed him throughout his life, but abused his mind the worst it ever had now that he was twenty-five-years old with his own house to maintain and a water leak that needed to be taken care of.

He moved away the piece of plywood that was covering up the opening to the crawl space, got down on his hands and knees, and peered in with the flashlight. It was dark, damp, and camel crickets hopped along cinderblocks and cobwebs dangled from every section of the floorboards. His anxiety immediately thickened just thinking about all the things that could go wrong while being wedged in such a confined space. He lay there for twenty minutes, going over every single terrifying scenario he could think of; but paying a professional hundreds of dollars for a cheap, simple DIY fix sounded even more horrendous. He now understood why his father always insisted on doing things himself—to save money.

His shaking arms pulled him forward as he made his way into the house's cavity after finally building up the courage. Inching his way through the musty darkness, he kept his eyes peeled, watching out for any unexpected surprises. He knew that what had happened to his father was a freak accident and the chances of it happening to him were very slim, but it didn't stop him from thinking about it as he made his way through the crawl space. He liked to believe that his father would have been proud of him for facing his fears—and a part of him liked to believe that he wasn't under that house alone, and that his father was right there by his side.

The busted water pipe had done more damage than he'd expected. The support beams had been soaking up the water like a sponge and black mold was starting to develop. Boards were warping, causing an unlevel surface in the dining room. He propped up his flashlight on a piece of sandstone, then grabbed the small notepad from his pants pocket and the pencil he had tucked behind his ear. He began jotting down a list of things he'd need from the hardware store in order to fix the unfortunate disaster. He needed a few new boards to trade out the rotted ones, distilled white vinegar to get rid of the mold, and a new water pipe to replace what had caused the entire catastrophe.

After ten minutes of gathering all the information that he needed, he slowly maneuvered his body to turn back around. He was more than ready to get himself out of that grimy place, but when he'd grabbed his light off the rock from where it had been sitting, it sent spiders sprawling out from a small nest beneath it. Spindly legs scattered in every direction and his beating heart became rapid as panic set in. As he dug his palms into the ground, quickly trying to force himself up to escape the trap that he'd put himself in, a screw sticking out of the floor board pierced through the back of his head. His eyes rolled to the back of his sockets, his arms collapsed, and he slowly slid off the bloody threads. His face came down with a smack against the corner of a cinderblock that was holding up one of the support beams, and he managed to roll over onto his back. Blood began puddling around his head, steadily flowing out of the open hole that the screw had left. His tiring eyes opened to the sight of small fragments of his brain that still clung to the screw, his own blood slowly dripping off of it onto his already swollen cheekbone. Everything happened so quickly that he could barely register the fact that it was definitely the end of him. And as darkness began to close in, the muffled sound of a voice above him from inside the house reached his dying ears. All was growing still as his life and senses began to fade, but in those final moments, he was granted a moment of clarity as to what the final words his five-year-old son spoke to him were.

"Daddy, you okay under there?"

You may think that the mess is simply chaos
I'm committing, the dirty deeds that only I
have the desire to fulfill.

I think of the mess as the inconvenient
evidence I'm forced to dispose of after my
doings are done, all because you don't
appreciate my fatal works of art.

I'll scrub the slate clean and save you the
concern; I'll allow you the ignorance it takes
for me to continue my dangerous ways.

Just know in the meantime that I'm doing this
for me, not because you're afraid of the
wicked things I do and say.

If you enjoyed these short stories, consider leaving this collection a review. Every bit of positive feedback helps to promote great stories to new readers.

Thank you for reading!

-Sonny March

Printed in Great Britain
by Amazon